My Book

by Jane Belk Moncure

illustrated by Linda Hohag

THE CHILD'S WORLD

ELGIN, ILLINOIS 60120

Library of Congress Cataloging in Publication Data

Moncure, Jane Belk.
  My "t" book.

  (My first steps to reading)
  Rev. ed. of: My t sound box. © 1977.
  Summary: Little t looks for toys beginning with
the letter t to put in his box.
  1. Children's stories, American.   [1. Alphabet]
I. Hohag, Linda. ill.   II. Moncure, Jane Belk.
My t sound box.   III. Title.   IV. Series: Moncure,
Jane Belk.   My first steps to reading.
PZ7.M739Myt 1984   [E]   84-17552
ISBN 0-89565-292-7

Distributed by Childrens Press, 1224 West Van Buren Street,
Chicago, Illinois 60607.

My "t" Book

(Blends are included in this book.)

Little  had a

It was a big box.

He said, "I will fill my

I will find toys."

7

Little  found a toy train.

He put the
toy train into his box.

Little  found a

toy tractor.

Guess where he put the toy tractor?

9

Then Little ✝ found a truck.

He drove the truck up, up,

up a tall mountain.
He drove to the top,
the very tip-top!

He found two turtles.

"In you go,
turtles,"
he said.

Then he
found
a toad.

"In you go, toad," he said.

Now the box was so full that he tripped.

Down, down he went.

He tumbled
into a turkey.

Turkey feathers flew.

So Little ✝ made a

turkey-feather hat.

He and the turkey danced.

Little  found a tom-tom.

He tapped the tom-tom,
"Tom, tum, tum."
Then he found a tomahawk

Little  and the turkey
danced some more.

Then he put
all his things
into the box.

box

Then Little  heard a terrific noise!

box

He ran into a teepee.

When he looked out, he saw a

tiger.

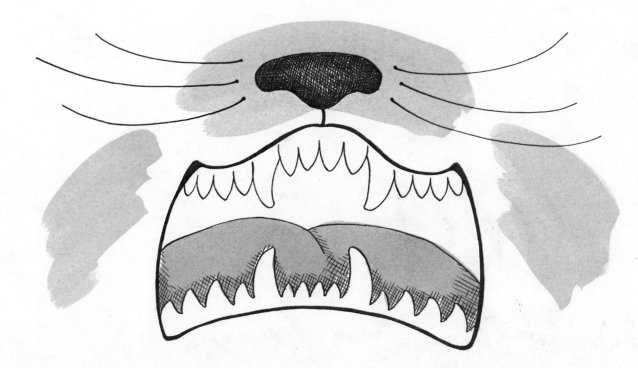

He saw lots of teeth
in the tiger's mouth.

"I have a loose tooth,"
said the tiger.
"Please pull out my tooth!"

24

So Little **t** pulled out the tooth.

box

Little 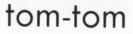 and the tiger played with the truck and the toys in the box.

tiger

toad

truck

tom-tom

26

rain track

mahawk

train

turtle

turkey

tractor

They had a
terrific time.

More words with Little .

telephone

tulip

tray

tricycle

toe

tree

tomato

toothbrush

television

tie

table

top

taco

tire

teapot

29